I0689952

Delbert A. Reynolds

A Scrap of Brown Paper

A Serio-Comic Drama in Four Acts

Delbert A. Reynolds

A Scrap of Brown Paper
A Serio-Comic Drama in Four Acts

ISBN/EAN: 9783337342166

Printed in Europe, USA, Canada, Australia, Japan

Cover: Foto ©Andreas Hilbeck / pixelio.de

More available books at **www.hansebooks.com**

A Scrap of Brown Paper,

A

SERIO-COMIC DRAMA

IN FOUR ACTS

BY

D. A. REYNOLDS

AUTHOR OF

"Wolverton, or The Modern Arena," "At Heaven's Window."
"Tangled Lives," etc.

1892
D. A. Reynolds & Co., Publishers,
Lansing, Mich.

SYNOPSIS OF ACTS.

ACT I.--Calling to supper—A hot day—Letter from Tom—A mishap—Goin' to York—Doing the churning—Setting the Hamburgs—A "misfit" SCENE 2—Streets of New York—Dempsy discovers an heiress—Lillian's dream—Andy's prescription—Andy becomes musical—A lover's quarrel—Passion's slave—Kate Field's slavery. SCENE 3--Mrs. Gibbon's parlor—Lillian's betrothal--Mary Ann expects company—A faithful spy—A seasoned kiss—"Ye've bin kalsomining yer face, Mary Ann"—Abduction of the heiress, Lillian Fairchild.

ACT II—Near Union Depot—Mr. and Mrs. Weed reach New York—Mrs. Weed discovers a real dude—Flirting under difficulties --Jack Dempsy's new plot—An unwilling tool—Automatic broom factory—"Hoigh livin' is it?"—Timothy Weed on "Kingsbury" rules--A "Galavanting old duffer." SCENE 2—A lover's anguish Andy's new master—"Lit me spit on me chip"—A hint of Lillian's captor—Dempsy's rage—"This thing talks widout spakin'" Timothy Weed's "store clos' "—A bountiful harvest—Stub on patent leather—Off for the search. SCENE 3—Lillian's captivity—The haunted chamber--Bread and water—Lillian's anguish—Kate Field's confession—Dempsy's rage—Lillian's defiance—One hope—A scrap of brown paper.

ACT III.—Trapping a Yankee--"Guess I'll take beer"—How to treat a lady—A new visitor--Bill Skinner's boy—Drugging the wine—Better than new milk—A scrap of brown paper—The deed of Weed's Hollar—"Shoot Burgoyne, yer gun aint loaded." SCENE 2—A musical dude--Andy's contempt—A bad cold in the head--The dude in a shower-- Mary Ann's jealousy—An impromptu duel --A good umbrella—Finding a scrap of brown paper. SCENE 3—Dempsy's determination—Kate Field's defiance and resolution--Dempsy's oath of vengence--"Strike, coward, if you dare!"—A frightened dude—"Only flirtin' a little me darlint"—Song: "Oi will an' Oi wont."—An alarm of fire—Lillian in the flames Tom Weed to the rescue—Arson and murder.

ACT IV.—Tom Weed's home—Mary Ann's soliloquy—Andy returns--"Scare me agin"—"Yer chicken is burnin' me darlint."—After the wish-bone--Home from church—The husband's welcome –Timothy Weed's proposal—The Dude and Kate Field as home missionaries—Andy's courage and long knife--The "Funny Musk" —Jack Dempsy's vengence--Dempsy in the toils—A scrap of brown paper.

PROPERTIES.

Extra large dinner horn, rake, whip, wash-dish, bench, baking dish, churn, headless barrel, table, chairs and sewing machine.

CAST OF CHARACTERS.

LILLIAN FAIRCHILD, A sewing girl—Heiress.
TOM WEED, A rising young New York business man.
TIMOTHY WEED, A wealthy Vermont farmer,
JACK DEMPSY, An unscrupulous attorney.
ANDY MAGIN, A happy Irishman.
* JAMES DORSEY, An Irish farm hand.
AUGUSTUS STEBBINS, A musical New York dude.
STUB, A news boy.
MARIAR WEED, Wife of Timothy Weed.
KATE FIELD, A fallen woman.
MARY ANN, A domestic.
* MRS. GIBBONS, A matron.
                    Officers and Servants.

* Doubles.

COSTUMES:

LILLIAN FAIRCHILD, Act 1, 2 and 3, Sewing girl; 4 Bridal Robes.
TOM WEED, 1, 2 and 3, Business Suit; 4, Full Dress.
TIMOTHY WEED, II Scene 1, Act III Scene 1 and Act IV, Extravigantly dressed in "loud store close" that are too short and small high stand-up collar, etc. All other scenes, attired in loose fitting farmers habit.
MARIAR WEED, Act I, As farmers wife; All other scenes, extravigantly dressed in loud collars.
AUGUSTUS STEBBINS dude outfit, including cane and umbrella
Other costumes immaterial.

ACTS AND SCENES.

ACT 1 Scene 1, Full Stage, farm; 2, ⅓ Stage, Street; 3, Full, parlor.
ACT II Scene 1, Full Stage, Street; 3, ⅓ Stage, Street; 3, Full, dungeon.
ACT III, Scene 1, Full Stage, Saloon; 2, ⅓ Stage, Street; 3, Full St.
ACT IV Scene 1, Full Stage, Tom Weed's home.

A Scrap of Brown Paper.

SCENE I.— *Yard in rear of farm house—Full stage, house R. Enters Mrs. Weed from house R, with large dinner horn, attired in kitchen habit.*

Mrs. W. (*Looking L 3*) I swan to goodness if that man hant started yet! It's gittin' so I have ter pull his nose off to get him to come to his meals and his ears off to get him away. I never seed such a man! I've blowed and blowed on this old horn 'till I can't only squeak. I've drained the taters, sot the table and had the tea a bilin' for mor'n an hour and he hant turned up yet. I'll call him once more and then if he don't come he can eat a cold supper, that's what. (*Puts horn to mouth and blows— horn gives fine, shrill noise—tries other end: horn squeaks.*) Oh yes you'll work that way! Drive a man away from home, I'll be bound! I'd like to have that tin-peddler by the ears once, I'd make him toot. (*Places horn under arm, places hands to mouth and calls.*) Tim-o-thie! (*waits*) Tim o-thie! Oh dear, how that takes my wind! (*Answer w thout*) Well now, you'd better whoo-pee; I've stood this tarnal fooling long enough. (*Fixes around stage, fills wash-dish part full of water and sits it on wash-bench and Ex. R*)

(*Enters Timothy Weed with whip and rake.*)

Tim. (*Laughing.*)I 'll be tetotally consarned if this aint one of the scorchers. (*Setting down whip and rake at gate and tossing hat toward bench—letter falls out.*) There, I swan there's that letter from Tom; guess I'll look it over here in the shade. (*Laughs, picks up letter and deliberately tears off end while he reads:*) Timothy Weed, Esquire, Weed's Hollar, Bennington County, Vermont. New York 3;30 P. M., ninety-nine –that is blotted sost I can't read it. Return after ten days—That's all proper. sost post masters wont keep and read 'em. (*Gradually backs around to wash-bench and sits down in wash-dish.*)

Enters Mrs. Weed door R with tin of biscuits.

Mrs. W, Oh! (*Sees Weed, screams, throws-up hands, letting tin fall.*) Timothy Weed, you're always doing things wrong end to!

Now see what you've done!

Tim. (*Wringing water from pants.*) How can I see, Mariar, I havn't eyes in my back.

Mrs. W. I should think you could feel!

Tim. Come now, Mariar, don't scold, taint you'se got to suffer. Its better'n sost I had my store clos' on. Git a rag and help a fellow out.

Mrs. W. How in the world did you ever come to do it, Timothy? (*Using apron in drying process.*) are you blind?

Tim. Why, just as I drove out the lane, who should come along down the hollar but Zib Cummings with that new roan o' hisu that he traded them three-year-old steers with Bill Skinner fer, an' handed me this letter from Tom—howbeit I reckon its from Tom from the postmaster's mark on't.

Mrs. W. I swan to goodness! A letter from Tom. Let me see it. (*Snatches at envelope.*)

Tim. Hold on, now, Mariar *Giving her envelope and keeping letter.*) Them biscuits wont be very warm I reckon.

Mrs. W. That's always your way, Tim Weed! You never let me see anything! I always have to come in like the fifth calf and take what's left, an them biscuits, too, they've stood in the oven for two hours watin' your motions and the taters are gittin' cold and the chores hant done and no wood split and no water brought and the cows aint milked and——

Tim. Oh, come, Mariar, give us a rest. (*reads*) "Sweetest girl in New York." I'll be tetotally consarned, Mariar, (*demonstrative*) Tom's goin' ter git married and wants us to come to the weddin.

Mrs. W. No! Your fooling! He aint, is he? (*Leaning over his shoulder.*) Shure as I live and to a young woman at that! (*Polishing and adjusting spectacles, reads.*) "Just twenty one on the day she will be my wife." Why, Timothy, that was just my age when we were married.

Tim. (*Relinquishing letter.*) Yes, and Tom's about my age. I hope he'll git as good a piece o' land as the hollar by the time he's my age. Ha, ha! Tom's a russler; he'll do.

Mrs. W. And I hope she'll be as prudent and savin' as I've been.

A woman can throw out with a spoon more'n a man can bring in with a shovel. I guess Weeds hollar wouldn't a been much if it hadn't been for my scrapin' an' pinchin' along. (*Folding spectacles and putting in pocket.*)

Tim. There you go again, Mariar; always harpin' on savin'. Just as if I didn't give you twenty shillin's out o' the cheese money.

Mrs. W. Yes, but didn't you take the egg money to pay Bill Skinner for that patent churn o' hisn?

Tim. Sposin I did what then, wont you git the good of it? But say, Mariar, let up on this preachin' and let's talk about goin' to Tom's weddin'.

Mrs. W. What! Go clear way off to New York? What would Tom say?

Tim. Well I guess it haint no further from here to New York than from New York here. I'm a goin' that's what!

Mrs. W. Now see here. Timothy Weed, you don't go to New York alone. I hant going to have you galavanting 'round the city unpertected. When you spect to go?

Tim. I'm goin' tonight. I've alars had a hankerin to take in the stockyards, and now is a good time. (*laughs*) Git on your Sunday fixins, old lady, We'll leave the chores for the hired man. (*Ex. Mrs. W. R — laughing immoderately.*) Egad! wont Tom be stunned when he sees his mother and me in our store clos'! I wonder where that boy is! (*calls*) Jimmie! (*laughs*) What'll the neighbors think when they find me and Mariar gone to New York! (*Looks off R 3*) Carnsarn that boy why don't he come; (*calls*) Jim! (*Answer without.*) Come here, you rascal, didn't you hear me call you?

Enters James Dorsey.

Jas. Sure, sor, I tho't you was snoring.

Tim. Thought I was snorin' did you? ha, ha! your a comical rascal. What was you doing out there?

Jas. Sure, sor, I was sortin' the small paraties from the banes for the chicken's breakfast in the mornin'.

Tim. Ha, ha! Thats good. Did you git them done?

Jas. No sor, I was a watin'.

Tim. Watin', what was you watin' for?

Jas. For that raise you was after givin' me gist before hayin' set in.

Tim. Oh, never mind the raise—

Jas. (*aside*) I'm not.

Tim. I'll see to that.

Jas. (*aside*) I'd like to see it.

Tim. How would you like to be foreman, Jim?

Jas. Would I be after gittin' ope at thra in the mornin' an' buildin' the fairs?

Tim. No, say half past.

Jas. An' milkin' siven cows and feedin' the calves before breakfast?

Tim. No, Briget could feed the calves.

Jas. An' drive the kickin' mare?

Tim. No, turn her out to grass.

Jas. An' do all the shores after dark?

Tim. Why, y-e-a-s, there's not many to do.

Jas. (*aside*) I should say not; (*aloud*) and ye'll raise me to eight dollars a month?

Tim. Oh, come Jimmie, (*Tapping him on the shoulder.*) you'r gettin' too hard on the old man. Listen, old boy; me and Mariar's goin' down to York to see Tom married an' I'm goin' to make you foreman while I'm gone, ha, ha! See old boy?

Jas. (*aside*) Yis, foreman and hindman. (*aloud*) I'll sai to the woruk. An' so Tom's goin' ter be married is he indade? I'll warrant she's a foin lady wid plinty or monay—a regular jerist.

Tim. You mean an heiress, Jimmie.

Jas. Divil a bit would I care, I'd marry one or thim as quick as the other if they ounly had plinty or money.

Tim. That's right, Jimmie, (*Slapping him on th shoulder*) Its money makes the mare go. Tom's a chip o' the old block ivery time. You wont catch Tom Weed marryin' a woman lest she's some bottom to her—No highfliers on his plate.

Enters Mrs. Weed, prtially ready.

Mrs. W. Timothy Weed, why on arth aint you gittin' ready? Here I am almost ready an' you hant begun. That's just the way with a man, you have to fuss and work with them a nour after you'r all ready. An' I don't bleve you've thought o' them Hamburg- since you got the eggs.

Tim. That's what, Mariar, an' the old yaller's been cluckin' 'round fer three days. Get the sittin' an' I'll go right out an' set 'er. [*Ex Mrs. W. L.*] Egad, I most forgot that—wouldn't had them eggs spilt for twenty shillin's

Enters Mrs. Weed with basket of eggs.

Tim. (*Counting eggs.*) Thirteen; that's right. (*Ex L. 3. calling back.*) Get ready, now, Mariar!

Mrs. W. I swan to goodness if that aint the worst man I ever did see! I believe he'd hurry me if he was going to be hung. (*To James.*) Here, Jimmie, do this churning for me, want you? [*Ex R 1*

Jas. O, yeas Oi,ll dew the shurning, Oi Will! Oi loike to spblader the crame all over me Sunday britches! Oi look loik it, Oi do!

Enters Mrs. Weed with churn and apron.

Mrs. W. (*Sitting churn R.*) Come, now, Jimmie, you'r a good fellow, and see I'll put this apron on you to protect yonr cloths. (*Puts apron on James.*)

Jas. (*aside.*) O yis, O'im a good fellow, Oi am. Bejabers Oi belaive they,d coax a fellow into slapping his grand-mother. (*Takes chair R and begins churning energetically*) Oi'm a toin dairy maid Oi am! [*Ex Mrs. W.*] (*Takes cream from dasher with fore finger and lickes it off.*) Its coming. (*Churns and repeats as before.*)

Tim. (*From without.*) Mariar—Mariar—I say Mariar—can't you come and help a feller out?

Enters Timothy Weed L 3 wedged into barrel—falls on stage and rolls toward front. Enters Mrs Weed R 1 doing up hair.

Mrs. W. Timothy Weed, what on arth you been doin'! (*Mrs. W. and James rush to his assistance.*)

Tim. That tarnal old yeller picked at me when I went to set 'er!

Jas. Ye've got a misfit this toim, sure! Oi should think the yellar had set you. (*Mrs. W. takes hold of Timothy, James tries to pull off barrel.*)

Tim. Oh! Nails.

Mrs. W. Grin an' bear it Timothy.

Jas. What goes in must come out.

SCENE 3—*Front third—Streets of New York. Enters Stub R selling papers.*

Stub (*Papers under arm.*) All about the Coney Island murder. Herald—Times—World—

Enters Jack Dempsy L.

Papers Sir? All about the races!

Demp. I don't care a flip about your races!

Stub Markets, Sir? Wheat gone up five points!

Demp. Here, give me a *World.* (*Tosses penny in street.*)

Stub (*Scampering after penny and going L. Looks over shoulder defiantly aside.*) I'll bet your a scamp, I do! [*Ex L.*

Demp. (*reading.*) "Joseph Fairchild a former Wall street operator who recently died in Australia, leaves his entire fortune to his brother s child, who left her New England home about three years since to earn her living in one of our eastern cities as a sewing girl. Fairchild is said to have struck a rich find on the big island." Fairchild—Fairchild—that name sounds familiar. Where have I heard it? Oh, I know; that's the young lady Tom Weed's going to marry, I wager a beaver. I think I'll look into this. [*Ex R*

Enters Tom Weed L.

Tom. (*Looking at watch.*) I declare its time that mail was delivered and I expected a letter from father.

Enters Stub with papers. L.

Stub Papers, papers, all about the—

Tom. Here, my boy, do you want to turn an honest penny? (*Gives him coin.*) Run down to my office and bring my mail over to me at the Exchange. Hustle now!

Stub (*Lifting hat.*) Yes sir. [*Ex L.*

Enters Lillian Fairchild R.

Tom. (*Going to meet her.*) Why Lillian!

Lil. Oh Thomas, I am so glad to find you. (*Taking both hands.*) I—I was afraid you was sick or—or something

Tom. (*Laughing.*) Why, darling, what should have put that into your head? (*Affectionately.*) What in this world *could* happen to me?

Lil. (*Embarrassed.*) I—I dont know, but I couldn't help thinking. I had such a horrid dream last night.

Tom. (*Laughin.*) A dream! well, I declare! What was it, little one?

Lil. And you wont laugh at me?

Tom. (*Laughing.*) Laugh at you? Why bless me? the idea that you should dream of me is enough to tickle me clear through.

Lil. (*Seriously.*) But Tom, I'm sure something is going to happen. I thought I was in a big, dark room and a big, dark, ugly man was standing over me with a sword in his hand; then I thought the house was on fire where you room and they wouldn't let me come to you. Oh, it was awful! (*Covering face with handkerchief.*)

Tom. There, there, Lillian;(*Taking her hands.*) Don't worry about it now. It would take more than fire to separate us, and if any big, dark, ugly man molests you, he he'll hear from me.

Andy Appears R.

Lil. (*Recovering.*) But Tom, don't you believe something in dreams?

Andy Praps ye've bin aitin' suthin' an' it didn't agra wid ye. If ye'll try catnip a bit, it'll help ut. Me maither alus gave it to us childers.   [*Ex Lillian L. embarrassed.*

Tom. That you, Andy? I thought you were taking a law course in Dempsy's office.

Andy (*Aside.*) A course at the divil's woruk. (*Aloud.*) Sure, sor, Oi'm too dacent a mon fer thot.

Tom. How's that, Andy. I thought lawyers were the pink of the professions.

Andy Indade the lawyers are not tha painks of mything. Sharp wons, are thricky, tha young wons are nippy, tha dull wons are no good at all; tha short wons are puffy, tha tall wons are bluffy, an' the ould wons will gobble it all.

Tom. You'll do, Andy, I see you have a good idea of the first principals of the profession (*Going R.*)

Andy I say, Mishter Wade, would ye be after telling ma tha name of thot fair leddy as was after warming yer hands gist now?

Tom. (*Hesitatingly.*) Oh! that was a lady friend of mine whom I happened to meet on the street. That was all. You should not be so observing. [*Ex. R.*

Andy Sure an' its a moighty foin girl one don't mate on the strates ivery day. Oi thank Oi'll drame of her ivery noight for a wake. (*Looking both diretcions.*) Sure Oi thot tha masther was comin'. He told me Oi should ba here prezacly at half post foive and here it is pretty near toim fer the shops ter lit out. Niver moin, Oi'll sing a song fer company loik. an' whin the pretty girruls come along Oi'll take a sly peep at thim, so Oi will. (*Sings. Enters Mary Ann R. with work basket. Coming slyly up behind Andy and hits him slightly on the ribs. Catches instinctively, breaking off in middle of last verse.*) Och! murther! Oi've got it! (*Swings round franticly, catches Mary Ann in his arms and gives her a kiss—gets a slap in the face.*) Och, darlint, ye've narley schart the loif out o' me. Sure Oi thot Oi was kilt.

M. A. An' so ye'd be afther kissin' the sword what kilt ye, would ye? Ah, Andy Magin, Oi know yer.

Andy. Sure, now, and whin did ye get yer introduction? (*Aside.*) Be gad Oi'm geittin' so I hardly know meself. (*Rubbing his face.*)

M. A. Did'nt Oi say ye winkin' at the pretty girruls this morn in'?

Andy Sure, Mary Ann Oi thot twas you.

M. A. Ah, to grass wid yer blarney! Did yer sai anything green in me eye? (*Puts finger to eye.*)

Andy (*Advances, looks into her eye, jumped back dramatically.*) Och, darlint its me own swate self thot Oi sai all the whoile! (*Catches her in his arms.*)

Enters *Tom Weed L.*

[*Ex. Mary Ann R.*

Andy, (*Confused.*) Will Oi guess Oi'll not wait fer ther mashter maybe he's got losht. (*Going R.*)

Tom. I say, Andy! Who was that young lady you met just now?

Andy. Niver you moin about that now. Its gist about a harse apace. (*Aside.*) He'll be afther thrading secrets wid me yit. [*Ex. R*

Tom. (*Laughing.*) What a queer world, where every man hides from his brother the noblest impulses of his nature, and blushes to acknowledge the divine spark that kindles passion, and sets the life blood coursing through his veins with renewed vigor.

Jack Dempsy appears L—dodges back.

Show me the man who ne're was passion's slave
And I 'will cite, an idot or a knave. [*Ex R.*

Enters Jack Dempsy L.

Demp. Just in time. Of all men I know, Tom Weed is the man I had rather *not* meet. Lucky fellow—going to marry an heiress and don't know it. If--(*Laughs scornfully.*) he don't miss it. (*Savagely*) No sir! Tom Weed! (*Shaking fist off R.*) while I live, you shall never marry Lillian Fairchild!

Enters Kate Field R.

Kate. (*Timidly coming forward.*) You here. Jack, I did not mean to keep you waiting.

Demp. (*Crossly.*) That's always your plea--you never "mean to." If you were going to be hung you wouldn't "mean to."

Kate. Don't scold me, Jack! see, I have only just returned from that young man's room you so cruelly led away last night. It was his first glass of wine, and now--

Demp. Oh shut up that preaching! The young fool ought to have known better. Did you get the money?

Kate. Yes, but--

Demp. Was he getting over his spree when you left him?

Kate. Oh Jack; how cruel you can be! If you could only have seen those flushed features, those blood-shot eyes and hear him calling the name of mother, I know it would have touched you.

Demp. Oh shut up. How much did you get?

Kate. This. (*Giving money.*)

Demp. Was this all he had? (*Counting it.*)

Kate. N-no, I left part— he looked so sick and bad—

Demp. You'r a nice one, you are! You'r getting mighty chicken-hearted of late.

Kate. (*Pleadingly.*) Jack, don't scold. I can't stand it. This life is killing me. I've went through everything for you, and it seems to get worse and worse all the while. I shall have to quit.

Demp. (*Affectionately.*] Oh, come, Kate, you are down-hearted to-night. That baby from way-back has made you timid. Only one more venture, little girl, and we'll call quits. I've struck the richest lead yet.

Kate. (*Dispairingly.*) Another scheme?

Demp. Oh don't be so tragic! This little scheme will only be a passtime for you, listen and I will tell you.

Kate. (*Resignedly.*) Go on.

Demp. I've just learned that Lillian Fairchild, the sewing girl, is old Joe Fairchild's heiress. Fairchild has just died in Australia, worth half a million, and it all comes to this girl.

Kate. (*Interestedly.*) Does she know of this good fortune?

Demp. No, but that's not all. She is about to be married to a hustling young business man of Park Place who thinks she is made of gold.

Kate. (*Suspiciously.*) And you propose to get her away from him and marry her yourself?

Demp. Nonsense, Kate, what are you thinking about! Nothing of the kind. The thing to do is to get this girl away and hide her until a reward is offered. The lover will go frantic, the papers will get hold of it, everybody will know she is the heiress, and we'll pocket the reward.

Kate. Where does she live? Have you learned all about her?

Demp. Yes, she lives with an old lady in one of the flats down near central depot, and I have arranged to have every thing in readiness to carry out our plans at ten o'clock to night.

Enters Andy R.

Andy. Bejabers it's not safe to walk along tha streets iny more fer fair ye'll run over a couple of doves billing and cooing gist as if all the rist of the woruld were blind as a beetle. (*Turns to go.*) Oi guiss Oi'll go and foind me darlint and have a little flirtation of me own.   [*Ex. Kate L.*

Demp. Hold on there Andy, I want to speak with you.

Andy. (*Aside.*) some more diviltry I'll bit. (*Aloud.*) Is it after spaking wid me that ye'r sayin? Indeed ye'll not foind a truer Irishmun if ye'd go the whole city over.

Demp. One of the real, simon pure kind, eh?

Andy. Will I should say yis: me father was an Irishmun, me mother was an Irishmun, all me brothers and sisters were Irishmun and myself was boruned in the country Tipperarie.

Demp. That's an exelent pedagree you have, Andy, and now I want you to do me a favor. (*Tossing him money.*) Do you ever take anything, Andy?

Andy. (*Looking at coin.*) Not very much on that, do ye mind.

Demp. Don't be extravigant, Andy; (*Confidentilly.*) You just keep an eye on Tom Weed tonight, and I'll double it next time. You understand? [*Ex R.*

Andy Yis, Oi'll kape an eye on 'im; and if the divil don't claim his own, I take it that some one'll kape an eye on yersilf. [*Ex L.*
[*Draws off to full stage*]

SCENE 3.—*Full stage—Mrs. Gibbon's parlor. Table R. sofa L. sewing machine rear. Discovers Mrs. Gibbons and Lillian seated sewing at table R.*

Mrs. G. So we are to lose you, are we Lillian? After the two years you have been with us, it seems like parting with my own daughter.

Lil. Yes, auntie, I think my days as a sewing girl are over. Thomas has bought us a neat little cottage, where we shall be as comfortable and happy as two little bugs in a basket.

Mrs. G. I sincerely congratulate you, Lillian, and rejoice with you in your bright picture of happiness. I think Mr. Weed possesses those sterling qualities of manhood that women admire in a husband.

Lil. Is it not strange that he should have chosen a poor sewing girl for a wife when he could have married in the wealthy circles of his business acquaintance?

Mrs. G. Mr. Weed has chosen the better part. He evidently desires a home where he can find rest from the exacting cares of his busy life, and a wife that will live for him rather than society.

Lil. And he shall have it if love and devotion on my part can secure it.

Enters Mary Ann extravigantly dressed and highly powdered.

M. A. (*Swinging into room and cutting circles.*)

Me lover is coming this avening,—

He's a foin, jolly fellow Oi'm sure:

Oi'll listen so swate to his blarney

And kiss him good-bye at the dour.

Mrs. G. (*Rising.*) Mercy on me Mary Ann, where are you going togged out like that?

M. A. Going is it? Sure Oi'm going to have company for meself. Did ye think Miss Lillian was going to have all the good things of this woruld?

Lil. (*Rising and shaking out garment.*) You do not envy me my happiness Mary Ann?

M. A. Divil a whit. me darlin, (*Coming up to Lillian.*) Mishter Wade is a foin young man. Oi think if he was only an Irishman, Oi'd be after setting my own cap for him, meself.

Lil. (*Laughing.*) I think your cap is pretty well filled already. You must be careful not to have too many strings to your bow.

M. A. Niver ye fear me darlint, it's bows to me string Oi'm afther gittin'. When one gets bent a bit, ye can take another, do ye moind? (*Knock at door.*) Sure, Oi'll bit me darlint's come aldready. (*Going to door.*) [*Ex. Mrs. G. R.*

Enters Tom Weed, rear.

M. A. (*As if to embrace him, then backs off.*) Sure Oi thot 'twas —twas—

Tom. Andy?

M. A. (*Backing off.*) Sure, and it moight have bin a worus wan. (*Going L front, turning back, covering face with hands and slyly peaking over right shoulder.*)

Lil. (*Greeting affectionately.*) Oh, Tom I am so glad you have come. We were just talking about you.

Tom. (*Taking both hands and leading her R front.*) Talking about me? Now that's nice: I hope it was not of my bad qualities.

Lil. Oh, indeed it was not.

Tom. (*Joyously.*) I thought as much from your bright and laughing eyes. But I have some good news for you Lillian; I just received a telegram from father tonight saying that he and mother would, attend our nuptuals.

Lil. (*In estacy.*) Won't that be delightful! Those dear old people! How much I have wondered what they were like.

Tom. (*Laughing.*) Yon will find them very primitive, but possessing kind hearts.

Lil. Oh. I know that: they could not be other than kind and generous, and be your parents. (*Knock at door, rear—Tom and Lil. rise*)

        Enter Andy, closing door and knocking on inside.

Andy. Sure Oi thot Oi'd come in and knock out. (*Coming forward to Weed and addressing him—Mary Ann L front evincing great delight.*) Sure sor, Oi'm glad Oi've found ye.

Tom. Found me? What in the world can you want with me? (*Laughing.*) You did not think I was lost I hope?

Andy. Naw, indade, ye're a great way from being losht wid two such pretty girruls wid ye. (*Glancing and winking at M. A.*

Tom. Am I wanted for anything?

Andy. Sure ye're wanted to kape out uf the hands o' the villian as is hirin' me to watch ye.

Tom. Hiring you to watch me? (*Laughing.*) Does some one think I am going to run away?

Lil. (*Evincing great fear.*) Oh. Tom! what does this mean? (*Covering face with hands.*) Oh. my dream, my dream!

Andy. Niver ye fear, me swate young lady, as long as Andy Magin is the fellow what's doin' the watchin'! Divil a hair of his head shall he harum while me name is Andy Magin.

Lil. Oh, thank you, thank you! But why should anyone watch him? Who is it that is plotting against us?

Andy. Indade its one of the divil's own. He gave me a quarther to watch ye's and Oi've aldready worrud out a good pair of shoes trapesing around afther ye.

Tom. (*Lauhging.*) Never mind, Andy, this will make up for what you have lost. (*Gives money.*)

Andy. God bliss the loikes of ye, and protect yer swate young lady from the harum of the bloody spalpeen. (*Edging off toward l. front—Tom and Lillian regain their seats.*) Mary Ann—Mary Ann I say! (*Jumps to kiss her; Mary Ann turns suddenly around—Spitting and wiping his mouth.*) Ah, Mary Ann, ye've been calsoming yer face.

M. A. (*Stamping her foot.*) No, Oi've not! That's some of the powther Oi bought at the sthore. That's Rose in Bloom.

Andy. Sure Oi thot 'twas tha lasht rose of summer. (*Looking at her proudly.*) Och, Mary Ann how swate ye'r lookin' this avening. (*Holds arms out to her.*)

M. A. (*Hesitates, and then rushes into his arms.*) Och Andy, how kin ye tempt me so! (*Puts up face for a kiss.*)

Andy. (*Turning face away—aside.*) One bite o' that's enough. (*Aloud.*) Did yer know, Mary Ann. Oi'm goin' to be a great millionair?

M. A. (*Very much interested.*) Naw, indade, Andy, (*Taking his hands.*) Where d yer git yer money?

Andy. (*Laughing.*) Money is it, me darlint? Is it not the wealth of yer swate self Oi'm gettin'?

M. A. (*Seating themselves on sofa.*) Ah, there ye go wid yer blarney agin. Sure ye've sold me fer enough aldready to buy a nate house on the avenue

Lil. Oh, Tom, do promise me to be careful of that bad, bad man. You know not at what hour he may work your ruin.

Tom. (*Rising.*) Never fear, little one, forewarned is forearmed. I am not afraid of the villian, and I hope you will dismiss all this worry fr m your mind. (*Taking both her hands affectionately.*) Remember, Lillian, this is the last time I shall call on Lillian Fairchild.—Tomorrow, darling, you shall be my wife. [*Ex. rear.*

Lil. (*Going to door and looking out after him.*) How happy I should be if it was not for this sad presentiment! He is so joyous in the anticipation of our union, and yet my heart tells me that he shall be taken from me. (*To Mary Ann.*) Mary Ann, will you please bring me a glass of water?

M. A. (*Rising.*) Yis mum.

Andy. (*Rising.*) Oi'll take cider if yer plaze.

M. A. (*Going.*) Ye will, wid ye?

Andy. (*Calling her back.*) Niver moin the cider me darlint; Oi ll take necter this toim, (*Kissing her.*) and be kapin' watch o' the mashter. [*Ex. rear*

M. A. Ah, the blagard, ha'll tase the loif out o' me, ontil Oi hive to say "yis" to be rid of him. [*Ex. R*

Lil. Oh, dear, 1 am so weary. (*Seating herself at table R and leaning head on hand.*) I wish the morrow was here and this terrible presentiment at an end.

Enter Kate Field and Jack Dempsey half masked door rear. Creeping up behind Lillian, she places sponge to her nose. Lillian jumps, screams, and falls senseless into the arms of Jack Dempsy.

QUICK CURTAIN

ACT II.

SCENE 1.— Full stage. *Street near Union Depot. Enters Timothy Weed with Mrs. Weed on his arm L 2. Both extravigantly dressed, carrying hand satchel, band box and umbrella—awkward.*

Tim. (*Looking up.*) Ill be tetotaly consarned Mariar if ther' aint a buildin' higher'n the peak o' my yellar barn. down in the back lot.

Mrs. W. And do see there, Timothy, someone's put their clock away up stairs in the winder, sost people'd know they had on'. I call that slingin' on style with a vengence.

Tim. Well, I spose it'd be kinder handy when a feller's workin' out in the back yard. but I shouldn't want ter climb up ther every night to do ther windin',

Enters Stub R 2. selling papers.

Stub. Papers, papers! All about the stolen heiress! Papers?

Mrs. W. Say, bub. who lives in the big house over there, with their clock up stairs?

Stub. Oh, kum off th' roof!

(*Mr. and Mrs. Weed jump and look where they were standing.*)

Tim.   Say, bub, what de ye ask for them papers?

Stub.   cent, cent and a half and two cents.

Tim.   Ye haint got the *Scrub Town Digger* have ye? (*To Mrs. W.* Kinder like to know what the folks think o' our comin' ter York.

Stub.   Oh' yer too soon!

Tim.   Well I guess we're sooner'n you are.   ,

Stub.   Go git the hay-seed out'n yer hair.

Mrs. W.   (*Brushing locks.*) There Timothy Weed ye' forgot to comb yer har, d idn't yer!

Stub.   Where'd ye git that hat?

Mrs. W.   (*Taking hat off and wipping trimming with corner of shawl.*) See here, young feller, I sold eggs and bide that hat, and if ye don't like it, ye needn't give me more o' yer sass.

Stub.   Oh, Rats!

Mrs. W.   (*Jumps and looks around.*) Oh, Timothy!

Tim.   Hant no rats here, Mariar; say, bub, d' ye live fer about here?

Stub.   Oh come off! Ye haint in it!   ·   [*Ex. L*

Mrs. W.   He is too! (*Catches coat and jerking it together; it pops open full length of back.*)

Tim.   There, Mariar, I told ye them store close warnt no 'count.

Mrs. W.   Well I swan to goodness! (*Takes pins and begins fastening coat.*)

Enters Dude L 2.

Dude.   (*Adjusting eyeglass and cautiously approaching and watching operations.*) Aw, I declawi; dose awful taylors—so prowokin'!

Mrs. W.   (*Turns head and sees dade—screams.*) Oh! Timothy, look! (*Tries to scare him.*)

Tim.   (*Jumping.*) Oh lord, Mariar, you've stuck that pin into me mor'n a rod! (*Tries to find pin in his back.*)

Mrs. W.   (*Flirting skirts at dude.*) S-h-h-h, s-h-h-h! Shoo! (*Dude acts timid.*) Here, Timothy, you hold this ban'-box an' I'll drive the critter off. (*Gives box to Weed and spreads umbrella. Dude spreads his umbrella, but continues to back off L 1. Finally turns and runs persued by Mrs. W.*)

Tim. Go it, old woman, you'll tree the critter if yer wind holds out! (*Laughing.*)

Enters Kate Field, R 2.

(*Bowing and scrapin extraviantly. Sets down grip and approaches Kate.*) How are ye, little one! Fine day! D' yer live fer about here? (*Extending hand to shake—Kate passes him by unnoticed and exit L 2 followed to screen by Weed, looking L 2.*) .I'll be tetotally consarned ef that girl haint deaf and dumn, and prettyer'n all git out! (*Backsto R loooking L 2, falls over grip and mashes bandbox.*)

Enters Mrs. Weed L 1.

Mrs. W. Timothy Weed what on arth have you bin doin'! (*Belables him with umbrella.*)

Tim. Nothin' Mariar,—I—I—I'm hurt. (*LookinL 2 .*)

Mrs. W. (*Gathering up remnents in apron and taking Weed by ear.*) Hurt are you? I'll hurt ye ef yer don't mind what yar doin'. (*Leads him R 1.*) I'll jist stop this galavantin', you bet.

Tim. Don't, Mariar! What'll people say? [*Ex R 1.*

Re-enters Kate Field L 2.

Kate. Oh dear, why don't he come! He said he would meet me here at nine o'clock sharp (*Looking at clock in tower.*) and here it is a quarter past. I almost wish he would never come; he is so changed. How affectionate and considerate he used to be; but now it is plotting, plotting, plotting. It almost seems to me at times that he has lost all love for me in his wild race to ruin. Ah. here he comes.

Enters Jack Dempsy L 3.

Demp. (*Affectionately.*) Ah, Kittie, have I kept you waiting? I declare. I had almost forgotten our appointment.

Kate. I wish you had.

Demp. Wish I had? Ha, ha! Why what would you have done if I had left you walking the streets in search of me while I was enjoying myself over a glass of wine?

Kate. I should have gone home and passed another night without added to the weight of sin now upon my soul.

Demp. O fudge! You've been attending the Salvation Army meetings and got salvation. 'Twont last Kate; better throw it off

like you would the spring fever and go in for something more tang-
able. By the way, Kate, how is our wild heiress?

Kate. She will die of grief. She will not eat and cannot sleep.
She walks her room and moans continually.

Demp. That's good; she will be an easy subject to manage after
she has come Tanner on it for a month or two.

Kate. Oh, Jack!

Demp. Shut up, baby; I did not ask you to come here to plead
for her; I have another place where I want to use you.

Kate. Yes, use me. That is all you care for me. If you can
use me to carry out some of your base plots, I am all right. (*Goes L 1.*)

Demp. Oh, come, Kate, the thing I have on now is a little
amusement for you. You see there is a rich old duffer in the city
from Vermont who is taking in the sights of the metropolis with his
old lady in great style. Now what I'm on, is to invite this old crony
out to a wine supper and show him some of the ways of the big city.

Kate. And me, what am I to do?

Demp. Oh come off, Kate; you know your part better than I
can tell you. Just as if the old duffer could stand the magnetism
of those eyes! Ha, ha; little sirene, you shall wear diamonds yet
if you only follow me. Tra la, little one!   [*Ex. R 2.*

Kate. I should sooner think it would be a set of bracelets; however, I suppose there is no turning back.

Enters Dude L 1.

Dude. (*With great affectation.*) Aw, ma dwear wyoung lady,
mawy aw have the gwate pleasure aw making you dwear awquain-
tance awe.

Kate. (*Severely.*) A wart on society!

Dude. (*Examining hand critically.*) Aw wawt, she said, on ma
soul, did I evar! The dwear chile is in erwor. (*Goes to Kate, is
about to kneel, brushes floor, blows dust off floor, lays down handkerchief and kneels.*)   [*Kate backs off and Ex.R.*

Enters Andy L 2.

Andy. (*Catches Dude by feet and gives him a somersault. Dude
regains feet and pulls out long whisk broom from back of coat and begins dusting himself.*) Sure Oi thot 'twas a dummy and its only a

jumpin' jack. Sai th' pacock dusting his fithers. (*Takes whisk away and returns L. Dude takes out another smaller broom and continues dusting.*) Sure this is a foin prisent fer me Mary Ann—the handle ish so schmall. (*Sees dude and takes away second broom. Repeats several times, brooms growing smaller. Finally makes examination of dude, and finding no more brooms, tumbles him off stage R 1. Gathering up brooms.*) Sure its tha firsht genuine automatic broom factory Oi ever did sai. (*Sticking brooms all over himself and prancing up and down stage.*) What koind of a jude would Oi make?

Enters Mary Ann R 2.

M. A. (*Watching Andy in estacy.*) Ouh, ouh, ouh!

Andy. (*Imitating dude.*) Sure me darlint would ye be after taking the loiks of me?

M. A. (*Taking him by the ear and raising him.*) None o' that now, me bie; Oi'll have no jude winkin' at me loik that now. Its a full grown mon Oi'll be after havin' or its meself Oi'll be 'till the wind blows me away.

Andy. (*Laughing and chucking her under the chin.*) Faith, me darlint, Oi belave ye'd reform the Church of Rome wid yer swate smoile.

M. A. And why was ye not calling after me the whole day long, whilst Oi've been looking the eyes out o' me?

Andy. Shure, Mary Ann, Oi have to take time to ate a bit!

M. A. And do ye tell ma now that yer livin' at the Grand Cintral?

Andy. (*Embarrassed.*) Indade, Oi—Oi—

M. A. Out wid it me bie; dount be ashimed of yer hoigh livin'.

Andy. Hoigh livin', is it me darlint, whin Oi take me nickle o' soup in the basement around the corner and coume up here to pick me teath?

M. A. And is that the way yer desavin'?

Andy. Sure, its the way all the bies are doin' and meself is only kapin' in the stoile. Gist wait 'till Oi git rich, and Oi'll be livin' on toads legs, so Oi will.

M. A. Is it rich yer telling me that ye'll be? D' yer main yer goin' to be an heiress. Andy?

Andy. (*Tapping head with finger.*) In me moind me darlint.

M. A. Ah, me bie, yer nairely bankrupt aldready ef ye did but know it. But why don't yer ax me to promenade wid ye? Haint Oi been waitin' this long time to be axed?

Andy. Sure, an' Oi've bin dyin' to ax ye all th' whoile. (*Tries to take her arm-while she tries to take his—Confusion ensues, both talking. Puts arm around waist.*) Oi'm always willin' to compremoise, me darlint; we'll not quarrel about that now.

M. A. (*Giving up with a show of great pleasure.*) That's gist the way wid the min, they always have the lasht worud.

[*Ex. L 1.*

Enters Timothy Weed R 2.

Tim. (*Setting down grip.*) I'll be tetotally consarned ef that aint just like they do up in the Hollar. I'd heard tell as how they had some new fangled ways down to York, but I guess its the same old story. *Opens grip and takes out large red bandana. Wipes face.*) By scratch I walked mor'n four miles to mail that letter and couldn't see the post master at that. Bet he won't know where its goin'!

Enters Jack Dempsy R 2.

Demp. (*Kicking grip—cloths, apples, popcorn, potatoes, ears of corn, etc., fall out.*) What have I found? (*Laughing.*)

Andy appears L 1, Dude R 1.

Tim. (*Grabbing Dempsy by collor and mopping stage with him.*)By scratch I'll show ye what we call it down in Vermont. (*Dempsy tries to get away. Weed holds him out with right hand and cuffs him with his old hat in the other.*) We call it flailin' down in Vermont.

Andy. (*Advancing and patting Weed on back.*) Give it to 'im old man with the roight fist, an' O'll stand at yer back. (*Gets a cuff of the hat in his face, Stagering off L 1.*) Och, Oi'm bloind! the ould machine is loaded at both inds.   [*Ex L 1.*

Dude. *Advancing and pocking umbrella into grip.*) Aw! Aw declaware! Quite wustic Aw must say! *Fishes out old sun-bonnet and puts it up aginst him with strings around him like apron.*) Aw! New style! wery unique, wery!

Tim. By scratch! Guess these folks don't know me! (*Reaches over for dude, doubles him up and sits down on him.— To Dempsy.*) Say, mister, just pick them things up inside of three jerks of a lamb's tail or there'll be a nuther wind storm around here. (*Dempsy hesitates.*) Hurry up, I feel it a comin'. (*Dempsy hustles things into grip and rushes off R 2. Releases dude, turns him around, looks him over and points R 2.*) Git! [*Ex Dude R 2.* By scratch! hant had so much fun fer a week. (*Looking around.*) Wonder if anybody else wants to try King-berry rules.

Enters Kate Field L 2.

Ah! There that deef girl agin. (*Closing grip and bowing extravigantly.*) My pretty dear, do ye live fer about here?

Kate. (*Simperingly.*) Yes sir.

Tim. (*Aside.*) I'll be tetotally consarned if that gal can't talk! (*Aloud.*) Little girl, how's yer ma?

Kate. I have no mother or father.

Tim. (*Affectedly—blowing his nose. Aside.*) By scratch I feel as though I could be a father to that gal. *Aloud.*) D' ye like candy little girl?

Kate. Oh, indeed, I'm very fond of it.

Tim. (*Aside.*) Guess I'll be her father yet. (*Aloud.*) Hold yer hat then—I'm alers kind to the widers and orphans.

Kate. (*Gathering up drapery.*) Oh how kind you are. Please put it in my lap.

Tim. (*Putting candy in lap.*) That's right, little girl. Always was kind hearted. D' ye like peanuts? (*Emptying pocket after pocket.*)

Kate. Oh, yes; and you'll come and see me sometime, wont you?

Tim. You bet I will. (*Aside.*) If I can get away from Mariar. (*Aloud.*) D' ye like bananas?

Kate. Oh, yes, yes; but you are too kind.

Tim. (*Piling up fruit.*) Don't say a word about it. And here is some ginger snaps I had left; and here is some apples I brought all the way from Vermont, and here--

Kate. Oh, please don't. My lap is running over now.

Tim. (*Taking large potato from pocket.*) There is that seed potater, now. Thought I'd lost it.

Enters Mrs. Weed L 2..

Mrs. W. (*Angrially.*) There Timothy Weed, that's just what I expected. (*Takes him by the ear and addresses Kate.*) Young lady, I guess yer mother wants ye and th' sooner you go the better! [*Kate Ex R 2.*] (*To Weed.*) You old galavanter, I'll keep my eye on you after this, see ef I don't. You'r a purty one to be flirtin' at your time o' life. (*Leads him off L 2.*)

[*Draws off to scene 2. Front third.*

SCENE 2, *Front third.—Enters Tom Weed R.*

Tom. (*Looking up from reading paper.*) Lillian Fairchild. an heiress and abducted! Great God! To-day she was to have been my wife! (*Reads.*) "In the hands of her abductor—possible murder!" My God, what awful head-lines! What can be done—what shall be done! Ha! I read her dream and will follow its direction. She is mine, dead or alive, and I swear by this strong arm that I will not sleep or rest while she remains in peril! (*Goes L and runs over Andy who is just entering L.*)

Andy. (*Hobbling about stage.*) Och, me carnes, me carnes! (*Holding up arm in imitation of Weed.*) Oi swear by the strong arm of me, that Oi'll lick iny mon that trods on me toes, so I will!

Tom. Why, Andy, my man, excuse me. I am in awful pain. (*Placing hand to heart.*)

Andy. (*Holding up one foot.*) Sure, and maybe ye don't think Oi'm in pain wid a corn on me toe as big as a murphy.

Tom. Andy, do you know that Lillian has been abducted?

Andy. (*Excitedly.*) Conducted is it! (*Spits on hands.*) Show me the bloody spalpeen that conducted her.

Tom. (*Reaching out paper.*) Have you seen that?

Andy. Sure that's the *Wourld:* ye didn't think Oi wanted the airth did ye?

Tom. (*Affectedly.*) Read it, read it: and tell me what heartless villian could have done this terrible deed.

Andy. (*Pushing back paper.*) Read it did yer say? Sure the bloody blarguard would be half the way to Yourup before Oi got the first loin spilt out. But Oi kin rade the moon, Mishter Wade.

Tom. Read the moon? What do you mean Andy? Tell me quick, my man.

Andy. Whoy, didn't ye know Oi was a clara voyant?

Tom. Clairvoyant? No. indeed.

Andy. (*Shutting his eyes and extending his hand.*) Sure Oi am thot. Gist tickle me hand and sai how quick the vision will come to me. (*Weed puts money in hand.*) Ouch, how that tickles! (*Takes a sly peep and sticks it into pocket.*) Sure yer enough ta make the angles laugh.

Tom. But lets have the vision.

Andy. (*Aside.*) Bejabers Oi almost forgot it. (*Aloud.*) Sure and if the divil was after ye, wouldn't he be afther takin' the bist holf of ye firsht?

Tom. Do you mean Jack Dempty? He could not have known Lillian.

Andy. Oi sid niver a worud about Dimpsy, but the divil always takes care ot his own.

Tom. Andy, you are a bright fellow and ought to serve a better master. Let me entreat you to leave this unscrupulous villian and assist me in the search for my lost darling.

Andy. (*Jingling money in pocket.*) Yer a foin mon, Mishter Wade and the swate young lady is the friud of me ouen darlint.

Tom. (*Excitedly.*) And you will help me Andy?

Andy. Wait a bit till Oi spit on me chip. (*Picks up chip and spits on it*) Droy Oi win, wit you lose. (*Tosses up chip and catches it in hand.*) Droy be jabers! Oi'll go ye one if Oi lose. (*Makes motion as if to toss chip toward audience, changes mind and throws it off R.*)

Tom. (*Holding up hand.*) Swear it, Andy.

Andy. Oi swear it boy the great corn on me shmall toe, that Oi'll niver lave ye so long as ye've got a dollar in yer pocket.

Tom. (*Gives money and a revolver.*) This is for you, and this is for our enemies. [*Ex. L.*

Enters Jack Dempsy L.

Demp. (*Angrially.*) So you have turned traitor, have you? How much do you get from your new master?

Andy. Half as much a gin wid me board throwed in; divide it in the middle and Oi'll take moin strait.

Demp. (*Sneeringly.*) You've become wonderfully cunning

since you've changed masters.   Hope he'll profit by your treach-
ery.

Andy.   Divil a whit would he profit out o' the loiks of yez; fer
the ould Nic has ye bought up body and sould.

Demp.   (*Advancing with raised cain.*)   None of your impudence
you Irish rascal or I'll thrash you on the spot.

Andy.   (*Presenting revolver.*)   Hould a bit!   (*Dempsy backs off
followed by Andy.*)   Git, wonst; git, twist; its a comin'—three toimes
Oi sai—(*Dempsy turns and runs off R.   Examining revolver.*)   Shore
that's a foin thing that talks widout spakin'   (*Revolver goes off in
hand.*)

Dude appears L.

Ouch, the divil! it spakes widout talkin!   (*Dude comes close to Andy
who picks up revolver carefully and frightens dude off L.   Tosses revolver after him.*)   Its a foin thing to drive off the varmint, but
Oi'll niver make me swate heart a widdy by the loiks of it.

Enters Mr. and Mrs. Weed R.

Tim.   Well, I'll be tetotally consarned if this aint the longest
street I ever went anywhere! Bin walkin' and walkin' four hours
an' hant got to the end on it yit.   (*Sits down grip.*)

Mrs. W.   Yes, and you will persist in going with then ol' duds
on—you do make me so shame!

Tim.   Good Lord, Mariar, ye dont spect me ter wear my store
clos' every day, do ye? (*To Andy.*) say, mister, do yer know where
a fellow could swop some right good land fer some o' these houses
think I'd like ter live in York, fer a fact.

Andy.   (*Laughing.*) Is it livin' in New Yoruk yed be after doin',
sure they'd havin' ye ope at the museum for an ould Puritan.

Enters Tom Weed L.

Tom.   (*Rushing forward.*)   Father, Mother! (*takes hand of each.*)

Andy.   (*Going L.*) Sure Oi gis the master's found sothin'; Oi'll
be after lookin' the ither way.   [*Ex L.*

Tim.   (*Advancing.*) By scratch if there aint Tom!·

Mrs. W.   (*Advancing and taking other hand.*) Sure as I live, an'
all dressed up as if he's goin' somewhere. (*To Tom.*) Bin, gone or
goin' some'ere?

Tom.   I was going to the depot to meet you and father. (*Looking at watch.*) Is the train in so soon?

Tim. (*Laughing heartily.*) Me an' mother's bin in town more'n a day. Come down a little a head, sost we could see sothin'. (*Critically looking Tom over.*) By scratch, Tom, ye must be makin' lots o' money to go togged out like that every day; (*Examining cloths.*) that suit never cost less'n fifteen dollars.

Tim. (*Smiling.*) Yes, it cost all of that father, but you haven't told me how things are doing at home, down on the farm.

Tim. Fust rate, Tom; never had a better year since we lived in the hollar. Hay good, corn bully, an old whoppin' crop o' buckwheat; and taters.--lord bless me! (*Feels around in pocket finds potato and exhibits it.*) had the biggest crop you ever did see! What d' ye think o' that fer a sample? Fer a fact, Tom, believe a lot of 'em 'd weigh ten pound.

Tom. (*Taking potato.*) I should not think it would take a very great lot of these to weigh ten pounds. I am heartily glad to hear that matters are doing so nicely, and to see you and mother look so well.

Mrs. W. Land sakes! Don'd think he looks well with them old duds on, do ye? But it ain't sost he didn't have a brand new suit o' store clos' he bought a year ago last fall in flax pullin' time. He's savin' 'em fer the wedin'.

Tom. (*Sorrowfully.*) Alas I fear he will never wear them.

Mrs. W. (*Anxiously.*) The gal hant gone back an ye, has she Tom? Tnese town girls —

Tom. (*Appealingly.*) Don't, mother, you do not know Lillian Fairchild, or you would honor all women for her sake. She is noble, generous and a queen among women. For two years she has been the guiding star of my ambition and the magnet of my success. Today she was to have been my bride; but cruel fate has robbed me of all I hold dear in life. She has been stolen away, possibly murdered; and I have not the slightest clue.

Tim. (*Excitedly.*) By scratch! This is gettin' interestin'! (*Wiping his face.*) I'll be tetotally consarned if I aint glad I come down —help the boy out. Nothin' like an old head on young shoulders fer this kind o' work.

Tom. But what can we do, father? The authorities are searching everywhere —— .

Tim. The 'thorities to grass! Spose I'm goin' ter wait fer them constables ter look 'er up? Not much! Tote yer mother off where she can be sort o' easy, and we'll strike out in dead 'arnest. (*Shoving Tom and Mrs. Weed off L.*)

Enters Dude R.

Dude. Aw! Quite wustic! Aw must say! How decidedly owiginal! Such a hat! (*Brushes own*) Mus' be f'om way back!

Enters Stub L.

Stub. Papers, papers! Papers sir?

Dude. (*Disdainfully.*) Naw!

Stub. (*Spitting on his shoes and passing R.*) Naw!

Dude. (*Jumping and wiping patent leather with handkerchief and looking angrily at Stub.*) How prowokin'! weally absurd! Never saw any fing like it in all my born days!

(*Stub crosses L., pretends to spit upon Dude's feet who tries to get out of his way. Re-crosses to R Driving dude off R trying to keep his feet behind him.*)

Stub. Oh, dear! No luck today. Guess I'll sing a song and see if it wont come back. (*Sings.*)

> All foot-sore and weary, I tramp through the street
> To offer my papers to each one I meet;
> And the pennies I earn buys the dinner I eat,
> For I'm spreading the news of the day.

CHORUS:—

> PAPERS! PAPERS!
> Oh I hustle through sun-shine, I hustle through storm,
> I hustle at night and I hustle at morn;
> Though I'm not quite in fashion, and not always warm,
> Yet I hustle for mother and me.

> I dodge the big bullies, fling off on the "rats,"
> I'm sweet on the fat girl that lives in the flat;
> She's got a big brother but who cares for that!
> For I'm spreading the news of the day.

CHORUS:—

Sometime I'll be "in it" as the newspapers say,
With plenty of money and nothing to pay;
Then I'll give all the news-boys a half-holiday,
Who are speading the news of the day.

CHORUS:— [*Ex. R.*

[*Draws off to Scene 3.*]

SCENE 3, —*Full stage—Darkened room—Table center, lounge rear—candle burned low—Lillian discovered with head bowed on table.*

Lil. (*Looking up wildly.*) Where am I—I must have fallen a-sleep! (*Looks around her and presses hands to temples.*) Oh, I remember! How cold, how dreary, how terrible! [*Rising, pacing floor, looking through iron shutters, etc.*) Alone, no friends, they have cast me away in this dark, dismal dungeon with not even the free light of heaven to cheer my aching heart. Am I a leper, that they should tear me away from those I love and place me where not even the sound of human voice shall cheer me! Am I an outcast whose very presence should pollute the pure atmosphere of the beautiful outer-world, lading it with the baneful scourge of unchastity, that they entomb me in this phantom dungeon without the whisper of hope or a kind message from those who love me! Am I a criminal, in whose frail hands should rest the bane of public virtue and private sanctity, that they should bind me within these dark walls with nothing but a black eternity to cheer my bleeding heart! (*The shadow of a hideous picture is reflected upon wall, rear.*) Am I mad, that they should turn these burning eye-balls in upon a parched and withering brain, that paints the fantastic forms of countless demons upon yonder wall, whose very image chills my blood and lays the icy hand of death upon my heart! Stricken by an unknown hand, turn from the very arms of one who loves me, my bridal robes are laid aside for these sombre garments of dispair whose every fold excludes each ray of hope nor bids me live to see the light of heaven. (*Kneeling.*) Oh, God of a bright and glorious universe, whose loving kindness

I was taught to lisp at my angel mother's knee, help me to bear
this crushing anguish and to feel that the ever triumphant march
of the base and wicked is not of thy will, but from the perverted
laws of thy generosity! Oh, Humanity, with all thy boast and
pride; with all thy vigilence and courage; with all thy honor and
philanthropy; why willst thou permit the stong to triumph in evil
and the weak to suffer! How can it be, that beneath the very
shadow of thy temples, bleeding hearts are daily and hourly send-
ing up their petitions for deliverance, only to pass like the wind
while you go on, on, in your revel, nor heed the base mockery of
your pretentions! Wilt thou, Oh, Humanity, pause in your wild
revel, long enough to register my petition and call forth the blind
Goddess of Justice to deliver me from this maddening throldom!
(*Noise rear—door slightly opens, bread and water passed in—Lillian
rises and stands pleading.*) Angel or demon, come into my solitude
and break this horrible silence that is turning the honey of my
soul into the vinegar of blasphema! Come with the light of mercy
in your eyes that bids me hope, or with the hellish grin of a spirit
damned to mock my brain into solitude of delirium! Any presence
however hidious, will banish this murky atmosphere that is slow-
ly, but surely stifling my cries and bearing me onward toward
the boundless shores of insanity!

(*Enters Kate Field rear, cautiously, fastening door behind her.
Lillian goes to Kate as if to embrace her, who retreats as if fearful of
her madness. Lilliad falls upon her knees.*) Oh my sister, have
you not come to banish the gloom of captivity and break the bars
that exclude the light of heaven! Have you brought with you one
ray of hope that shall banish this endless night! I see the light of
pity in your eyes, while your lip quivers with the kind words that
rise from your heart and demand a hearing! Speak, speak; my
hungry ears beat wildly for the sound of human voice and my
heart is bleeding for one grain of sympathy! Tell me, you who
bears the form of my angel mother, that your heart is not made of
stone, or that God has bereft you of speech as he has me of happiness!

Kate. (*Taking water and bread from floor upon a scrap of brown paper, setting them on table center.*) Miss Fairchild, your pleadings touch my heart, but I am utterly powerless to aid you. I am no less a prisioner than yourself, while the walls that bind me have all the blackness of sin and polution. You must bury your heart-aches as I have mine, and sustain life with the meager food I am permitted to bring you.

Lil. (*Rising and taking her hands.*) God bless you, my sister, for those words of sympathy. They come to me like a voice out of the darkness and bids me hope. But tell me what I have done that should banish me from all I love and place me in this dismal cell.

Kate. (*Leading Lillian to table and arranging food.*) The fault is not yours, Miss Fairchild; but the dire necessity of a wicked world. Let me entreat you to be calm and sustain your sinking nature by partaking of a little food.

Lil. To my famishing heart you offer me only the food that will prolong its suffering! Tell me, tell me something of your bond ge, that by the bonds of misery I may extend to you that sympathy which my heart so much craves!

Kate. I cannot tell you, for the very depth of your pure nature would not let you understand. How can you, in all your innocence, sympathize with me, chained as I am by the galling links of love, to a man whose noblest impulse is deceit, whose pride is cunning and whose ambition, plunder. Urged on by a wicked ambition and finding my love a means within his reach, he has pushed me before him down the plain of infamy, until today, that Love is sharing its throne with Fear, an abject slave to his tyrant hand.

Lil. And do you love him yet?

Kate. Love him! His very name sends a thrill through my being, while the light of his eye causes my blood to rush in torrents through my veins. The very thought that another may win him, sets my brain on fire, blinds me to all purity and goodness and renders me fit for the most hellish work it is possible for his dark mind to conceive.

Lil. Knowing him to be bad, would you marry him and thus perpetuate your slavery?

Kate. Marry him! Lives there a woman who would not marry Jack Dempsy, with all his faults?

Enters Jack Dempsy, rear.

(*Lillian and Kate start suddenly as if surprised.*)

Demp. (*Angrilly.*) Jack Dempsy with all his faults is amply able to take care of himself. (*To Kate.*) Is this the way you obey my orders? Go to your room this minute and stay there until I come. I can settle my own business with this young lady without your intercession. (*Kate starts for door rear and Lillian tries to intercept her.*)

Lil. Oh please don't go and leave me alone with this bad, wicked man!

Demp. (*Forcing her back.*) Back to your place you wildcat! I'm master here. [*Kate hesitates and finally Ex. rear.* You will learn after a while that I am in complete authority here and that all the opposition you can offer but adds to your discomfort.

Lil. (*Defiantly.*) Is it possible that one so utterly bereft of manhood as to offer violence to a woman can claim even the semblance of authority? Tell me, rather, that in your despotic madness you have violated every law of God and humanity to wreak vengeance upon one who has never injured you!

Demp. Your insolence wins for you the frankness you shall receive, and I will begin by telling you that you are as powerless to escape as if you were in the innermost cell of the tombs. This is my little kingdom where none dare question my authority, and where I am gracious only to those whom I will.

Lil. But what have I done to bring the power of your wrath down upon me?

Demp. (*Smiling sneeringly.*) Inadvertantly, Fate has allowed the lines of our fortunes to cross, and in some way they have become wonderful'y tangled. I have come to you to offer a solution which I hope you will carefully consider. I will not insult your good taste by a declaration of love at this inopportune moment, but will frankly confess that a union of our destinies appears inevitable. (*Lillian starts, but sustains herself by chair.*) Sometime, after the present emergency has passed, I may be able to convince you of the absorbing devotion that has prompted me to take this extreme measure.

Lil. And this is the ransome your base, scheming heart has placed upon my deliverance! After snatching me from the arms of him, who, thank God, has a right to protect me, and subjecting me to every discourtesy and torture it is in your wicked heart to devise, you come to me, the promised wife of one of God's noblemen, and dare to in ult me by offering me a position by the side of which a m id-house would be a paradise! Go to her you have, but just banished from your presence, and consecrate to her what little heart— what little manhood you have left. She, blinded by the love of what you might be, may be able to rekindle the spark of fidelity yet within you, and s ive you from your accused and profitless life.

Demp. (*Stepping forward.*) Do you dare refuse my offer and cast back upon me the ravings of a simpering fool? Do you realize your position?

Lil. Yes, and dare you to do your worst! Though seemingly within your power, I am as much above you as the heavens are above the earth! Your brusk bravado, calculated to intimidate helpless cripples and defenceless women, has no terror for me! Your cringing soul dare not tempt you to violence, and I defy your lying tongue to do me injury!

Demp. (*Stepping forward with clinched fist— Lillian raises chair Dempsy backs.*) Curse you, women! I will grind you to the earth! You have dared defy me within the very walls where I reign supreme, and I swear by the God of destiny that you shall drain the dregs of sorrow and despair to the last drop. Till then, I leave you in your mad folly to cry for pitty to these haunted walls! [*Ex.*

Lil. (*Rushing to the door and tries to make her escape. Rushes from door to window, tries to raise sash, fails, breaks glass out of window with hand and tries shutters.*) My God! My God! What shall I do! What new torment is in store for me! Is there no hope —Oh, what can I do! (*Sees paper on table, snatches it up, bread falls on floor.*) One ray of hope—One chance for liberty! (*Burns match and writes on paper. Coal wears off chars etc. Reads as she writes:*) I'M IN AWFUL PERIL! IN GOD'S NAME HELP ME! LILLIAN FAIRCHILD). (*Rushes to window, tucks paper through shutters —returns toward table.*) Oh dear, how dark, how—(*Swoons and falls on floor. Dempsy appears window rear--waves scrap of brown paper.*

CURTAIN.

ACT III.

Scene 1.— Full stage. *private parlor in fashionable saloon*. *Kate Field discovered at table center, reading.*

Kate. (*Laying down paper.*) Oh, dear, I wonder why that old duffer don't come! Every moment seems like an hour, so crowded is my vision with the phantoms of the past. I feel at times as if armies of angles and demons were contending for the possession of my soul, while I am boare on v rd, the victim of a bli d destiny. (*Noise rear.*) Hark! I hear him coming! (*Rising and going to door rear.*)

Enters Jack Dempsy rear.

You Jack, I thought this was to have b en a private affair?

Demp. Oh, that is all right; only you have been so chicken-hearted of late that I thought I would call early and give you a little cheering up befo e the old fellow showed up. You must remember that we are playing for desperate stakes tonight.

Kate. What do you expect to make out of this old countryman? I warrant he has not a dozen shillings in his old rags.

Demp. Oh yes he has; his pockets are lined with bank notes, besides, a whole valley up in Vermont to say nothing of a liberal bank account. (*Exhibiting legal paper.*) You see I have not been idle all this time, and am only waiting to get the old fellow mellowed up a little to make a good haul. By the way, I almost forgot to give you that medicine. (*Givin g paper.*) Use it sparingly, as we don't want the old fellow to go off on our h nds.

Kate. Oh Jack! Why will you lead such a life when you might——

Demp. There go again with your baby act! (*Knocking at door rear.*) Ah, there is your company. I will step in here and watch through the key-hole to see how well you carry out the program.

Ex L. 2.

Enters Timothy Weed, Rear, in "store clos."

Tim. I'll be tetotally consarned ef this don't look like home! D' ye live here right along, or kinder stay here an' take yer meals out on the street s mewhere?

Kate. (*Setting chair left of table for guest and seating herself right.*) Oh, I live further up town but came here to meet my friends.

Tim. (*Taking chair.*) Well now that's real nice; how much d' they charge fer a room like this?

Kate. Oh, they make no charge for the room; that all comes in with the refreshments.

Tim. Well I'll be tetotally consarned if I don't go an' engage rooms fer me an' Mariar at the same price! (*Examining call bell.*) What's this new fangled sheep-bell doin' on the table here? (*Bell rings and servant appears L. 1.—Weed looks up, sees servant and jumps up.*) What in thunder do you want in here?

Servant. (*Bowing.*) Orders. sir, orders?

Tim. (*Threateningly.*) Orders, you black raskal! By scratch, I'll give ye orders. (*Begins to take off coat.*) I'll show ye that ye don't come in here snoopin' around when I'm entertain' a young lady!

Kate. (*Trying to pacify him.*) Why dear Mr Weed, the man wants to know what you want in the way of refreshments. (*Helping him on with his coat and seating him.*) You rung the bell and he has only come to see what you want.

Tim. Well I want ye ter get out o' here in three jerks of a lamb's tail or I'll take my number nine from ye too quick!

Kate. But, my dear Mr. Weed, are you not going to order some refreshments? I would like a bottle of wine.

Tim. Oh well, ef ye have a hankerin' arter anything have him bring it a long.

Kate. But you have not given your order yet.

Tim. Oh, well I guess I'll take beer ef you've got some 'at's good. [*Ex servant.*] Gosh all hemlocks! I'd a had that feller licked in about a minit ef you hadn't set in.

Kate. You seem to be quite a stranger in the city!

Re-enters servant L 1. Bringing server, bottles, glasses, card of fares.

Tim. (*Picking up ticket.*) Gosh all hemlock! Six dollars for them two bottles? Can buy more'n a whole case o' beer in Scrub Town for that, young man! Hant ye got a smaller size fer. less money? (*Servant shakes head.*)

Kate. Why my dear Mr. Weed, I think that is very reasonable.

Tim. All right, let 'er go! Guess it wont break the bank. (*Is *about to pay servant, is stopped by Kate who motions him to put his money into his pocket. Grabs bottle, shakes it and is about to pull cork Kate and servant fearful of explosion—Cork comes out and strikes servant in face who retires in confusion L 1.*) I'll be tetotally consarned ef the blamed think wan't loaded! (*Kate puts powder in Weed's glass, and fills her own with wine and begins sipping it.— Weed is about to pour in glass when discovers powder.*) How tarnal slack these boardin' house woman are! Bet that glass haut been washed fer more'n a month! (*Empties powder from glass, wipes it out with coat tail, and drinks from bottle. Makes up awful face.*) Well now, ef they call that good down here. I'd like to have 'em get a swig of the stuf we have up in the hollar.

Enters Jack Dempsy L. 2.
Both rise, Weed eyeing the intruder with suspicion

Demp. (*Enthusiastically.*) Why if here isn't my old friend Weed from Vermont! How do you get along Uncle Timothy! (*Taking hand and shaking it.*) Why when did you come down—Saw your name in the city papers, but didn't know just where to look you up!

Tim. (*Appering to fall into the game.*) That's so, son of my old friend Bill Skinner who used to live over in skinner's Hollar, sure as I live! Why, Sam, how are ye! (*Shaking hands with a vengence —Dempsy winches and tries to pull away. Continues shaking.*) I'll be tetotally consarned ef I aint glad to see ye lookin' so well!

Demp. (*Getting his hand away and drawing up a chair to the table, all seating.*) Never felt better in the world, Uncle Timothy; making money hand over fist! (*Rings bell violently.*) Lets have some more wine—han't had a drop today.

Tim. Hem! yes, guess we had better. You buy this one—comes a little high!

Enters Servant L R.

Demp. Best Burgunda and glasses for three. (*Ex Servant. To Weed.*) By the way, Uncle Tim., have you struck anything rich since you come to the city? You used to know pretty near where all the loose dollars lay around Scrub Town, you remember. (*Enters servant L 1 with order sets it down and retires L 1.*) Guess I'll have to take you around and show you the city a little. (*Pours out wine in three glasses, slipping powder into one. Hits beer bottle with elbow and knockes it off table. Dempsy and Kate both stoop to get it—Weed reaches over, changes glasses and holds wine up to light.)* Oh, that's the genuine article, Uncle Tim., been here before! (*All touch glasses.*) Here's success, and that we may long live, love and be happy! (*All drink.*)

Tim. (*Smacking his mouth!*) By scratch that's fine! Guess I'll have another glass! (*Pours out more wine, drinks it off and smacks his lip.*) Gosh all hemlock! Han't had anything so good as that since the cows come in. (*Takes up bottle, holds it toward light, shakes it and drinks what is left. Dempsy shows signs of unconsciousness. Kate watching Weed, Weed rising.*) Say, young lady, aint it about time ye was agoin' hum? Maybe yer ma wouldn't like ter have ye out late ef she knowed where ye was. Taint no place fer a young gal and its time ye was agoin'. My young friend here has got drunker'n a fool an' I'll gest step ter the door and have one o'them blue coated constables come and carry him out. (*Kate hesitates.*) Come now, mosy right out, or maybe they'll want ter take ye along t r identify 'im. (*Takes Kate by shoulder and gently pushes her out rear.*) I'll be tetotally consarned ef things don't change around here quicker'n the weather in hayin' time. Guess I'll look this feller over'n see if he's got anything 'at might hurt 'im. (*Finds revolver, extracts balls and puts them in his mouth.*) Bill Skinner'd never let his boy carry shootin' irons around like that, and I know it. (*Puts revolver back and searches pockets; finds scrap of brown paper. Holds it to the light and tries to read.*) Durned poor writin, I call it, but maybe's the best he could do. (*Reads.*) "I'M IN AWFUL PERIL; IN GOD'S NAME HELP ME. LILLIAN FAIRCHILD." I'll be tetotally consarned ef I don't b'live Tom'd like to see that. (*Sticks it into pocket-Dempsy shows signs of returning consciousness.*) Took kinder a short nap after all, but I reckon it'll do 'im good.

Demp. Where am I? (*Rubbing his eyes and head.*) Have I been asleep? Heavens! How my head aches!

Tim. Guess that wine was a little to much for ye; er maybe ye got hold of the wrong glass. I feel bully! (*Holds up bottle and tries to get the last drop.*)

Demp. (*Jumping up.*) By heavens, I've been drugged! (*Places hand to pocket, draws out legal paper with one hand and revolver with the other. Throws paper upon table and points revolver at Weed.*) Sign that paper this minute or you are a dead man!

Tim. (*Deliberately unfolding paper and looking it over. Looking up.*) Why, Gosh all hemlock, that's a warrantee deed o' Weed's Hollar! Why that farm's worth a heap o' money young feller!

Demp. Will you sign that paper or die?

Tim. Can't do it, young feller; don't want ter sell the hollar no how.

Demp. Sign that paper, or when I say three, you die! One— Two—

Tim. (*Leaning back and folding his arms.*) Shoot, Burgoyne, yer gun aint loaded !

Tim. Three! (*Fires; Weed takes ball from mouth and tosses back at him. Repeat six times. Dempsy turns and rushes off door near.*)

Tim. Gosh all hemlock! How that pistol must a kicked! (*Laughs immoderately.*)

[*Draws of to scene 2.*]

SCENE 2—*Front third—Street. Enters Dude L. adjusting eyeglass, swinging umbrella. Goes R. turnes, passes back and forth across stage.*

Dude. How butufully butuful! Quite th' poppar fing Aw declawr! Wonderful pomenade! Aw wagor thar's mor'n forty putty gwirls lookin' at me this wery minute! Aw how wery propper. Aw only had a little muzic! Aw declawr Aw could sing. (*Music starts up; Sings.*)

> Aw'm quite aw catch so people saway,
> For Aw win thwar hawts wi' ma takin' way;
> But m i tailowr bills, Aw never pway—
> Thewr sent to ma paw in Brooklyn.

CHORUS:— Aw walk th' stweets wi' ma little feet,
Aund fix ma eye on all Aw meet;   (*Adjusting glass.*)
But th' way thway stawr when Aw chance to speak
Is tewrribly awfully awful.

Aw'm weally one o' th' uppor qwost—
Aw spwort ma cain wi' an awful wush—
But wot would Aw do if ma paw should bust.
Fwor Aw live wi' ma maw in Brooklyn.

CHORUS:—

Ma gloves ar' of th' pwopper shade,
Th' latwest stwile is all th' wage; (*Spreads pantaloons.*)
An' thwat twerrible bill thwat the twalor made
Was paid b' ma paw in Brooklyn.

CHORUS:--

B'hind th' scenes Aw'm quite a wake—
Aw pay all the bills thwat th' dwear ones make;
An' ma sweet mustach is an awful twake
Wi' th' dwear sweet gwirls in Brooklyn.

CHORUS:—

Enters Andy R.

Andy. (*Taking off dude's little hat and placing it upon his own head, own hat under arm—Dude looks in constarnation while Andy passes L and R.*) Ouch, its tirribly orfully orful!

Dude. How twerible; Aw do dweclar! Quite absurd.

Andy. (*Placing his own hat upon the dude's head.*) Sai how ye'd look wid a mon's hat on yer head! (*Laughing extravigantly.* Sure, it'd take more'n a mon's hat ter make a mon of yez! Ye'd have ter be milted op and run over agin before ye iver come to that!

Enters Stub L, makes motion as if to spit upon Dude's feet—Dude jumps—Stub Ex R.

Andy. Ouch, Oi belaive thot hat is givin' ma a big could in ma hid. (*Changes hats and sneezes.—Dude jumps violently. Repeats sneezing until dude is driven over foot-lights corner staje R. Dude spreds umbrella and couches under it as if in a storm. Peaks over umbrella.*)

Enters Mary Ann L.

(*Going to meet her.*) Ouch, me darlint, Oi was gist thankin' of yer own swate self this very minute.

M. A. (*Doubtfully.*) Was it of meself yer was thankin' and narely breakin' yer neck noddin' to the pretty girruls over there in tha corner?

Andy. Sure, me darlint, Oi got somethin' fast betwixt me eyes.

an' Oi was sneezin' it loost.

M. A. (*Sticking fist between eyes—Andy jumps back.*) Washt it loik that?

Audy. Ouch, Mary Ann, ye've thrown a whold handful of stars in me eyes. Oi'll niver snaze agin asht long as Oi live! But Mary Ann!

M. A. (*Looking other way.*) What shall oi say, me bie?

Andy. Hident ye bather kape yer sthrength for palin preaties?

M. A. Niver ye moind about that, me bie! Oi kin pale more than preaties wid me fisht. But say, Andy, where is Mishter Wade?

Andy. (*Examining nose.*) Gone.

M. A. Gone whire?

Andy. (*Rubbing nose violently.*) Crazy.

M. A. And hisen't he found the misthriss yit?

Andy. Niver a worud has he heard at all, a' tall; but ha's after the bloody blarguard thot conducted her.

M. A. Substracted her ye mane, Andy?

Andy. Divil a whit' do Oi care how she wint, sha's not been found yit ouyhow.

M. A. And what are ye doin' here, Andy, that yer not halpin' the mashter?

Andy. Sure Oi'm feastin' me eyes on yer own swate face, so Oi am.

M. A. (*Rushes off L.*) Niver a whit o' yer blarney will Oi haive agin 'till ye foind the mishtress. Go be a mon, Andy, and niver slape till ye've run down the spalpeen that stold her awey.

Andy. (*Watching her off L.*) Sure, me darlint, It's a big job ye've been givin' me, but Oi'll tackle it like a mon. [*Rushes off R sneezing at dude in passing.*

(*Dude cautiously creeps back on staye with umbrella partly spread, looking around him for danger. Dempsy appears R, Tom Weed appears L. Both draw revolvers. Dude rushes R then L very much frightened. Finally drops upon knees center and raises umbrella. Dempsy and Weed fire simultaneously.*)

Enters Mr. and Mrs Weed R.

(*Dude rushes back to hiding place. Mrs. Weed takes after Dempsy and drives him off R. with umbrella—Mr. Weed takes weapon from Tom and sticks it into his own pocket.*)

Tim. I'll be tetotally consarned ef this ain't as good as goin' ter see the cow-boy show down to Scrub Town last summer! Is, fer a fact! Hadn't orter fool with them shootin' irons, my boy; knowd a man that got hurt wonst.

Mrs. W. (*Coming up excitedly.*) Why Tom, ye mount o' hit 'im, and then what'd ye say?

Tom. I should say I had rid the world of a base, heartless villian.

Tim. Guess that's all right, Tom; but ye'd better do it at gov'ment expense.

[*Dude examines umbrella and wipes it off with har.dkerchief. Approaches Mrs. Weed who turnes on him and scares off R.*

Tom. I believe that man to be the abductor of Lillian Fairchild.

Tim. I'll be tetotally consarned ef I don't guess yer about level on that, Tom! (*To Mrs. Weed.*) Here, Mariar, hold yer apron and see ef I've lost that paper. (*Unloads all his pockets and finds scrap of paper.*) There, by scratch, I knewed I hadn't lost it. (*Handing paper to Tom and re-loading pockets.*)

Tom. (*Reading.*) "I'M IN AWFUL PERIL! IN GOD'S NAME HELP ME!" Great God, this is from Lillian! [*Rushes off L.*

Tim. (*Following.*) Hold on, Tom; an' me and yer mother'll go along! [*Both Ex L*

[*Draws off to full stage scene.*]

SCENE 3.—Full stage. *Converging from L. rear and R. rear, Enters Jack Dempsy R 2.*

Demp. (*Pacing to and fro and looking L. 2.*) Not here yet, and she is uasually so prompt. I don't krow what has taken posession of that girl lately; she seems to block my wheels in every way I am a mind to turn. Zounds! I half believe at times she's jealous! H i, ha! well, I don't know but she has a right to be; half a million dollars aint picked up every day, to say nothing of a sprightly young wild cat thrown in. First I'thought I'd keep the girl till she'd give in, and then offer to settle with her for half, but the more I've thought it over, the more I've changed my mind, and I guess I'll marry her, fortune and all. Wonder what Tom Reed would say to that! (*Looking at match.*) Confound that girl, I wonder what's keeping her! It seems that everything goes against me of late! Ah, here she comes now.

Enters Kate Field L 2.

Hello, what kept you so?

Kate. I could not come before.

Demp. Why? Anybody there?

Kate. No one but Miss Fairchild.

Demp. So you've been talking with her again, have you? Didn't I tell you to keep away from her?

Kate. What if you did?

Demp. What if I did! Haven't I a right to talk to her if I want to?

Kate. No sir; not for the purpose you have in view.

Demp. Who is it that dare challenge my right to talk to her when, where and how I choose?

Kate. She, the man that she has promised to wed, God and Justice.

Demp. And you—haven't you something to say about it?

Kate. No! There was a time when I claimed your promise that I prized as the highest gift of my inheritance; and when even the thought of your inconstancy would have driven me to madness. But that is past, and I have come here to tell you that I no longer love or fear you. You came to me in my purity, and taught me to love you. I believed you to be what you pretended—the soul of honor. You took all and gave me nothing in return. You lured me from home and friends, and filled my life with shame until I could no longer claim a place in their hearts. You have dragged me down, down into the sloughs of crime, and now you cast me off for your new victim. But Jack Dempsy, Lillian Fairchild will never succomb to you tyranny, or link her life to one so utterly deprived of everything that goes to make up manhood.

Demp. (*Advancing with clinched fist.*) Shut up this hellish jealousy or I will choke the words down your throat. What do you suppose a man in my position wants of a woman of your standing in society! What lady of position would open her doors to Kate Field, the street woman; and what pride I would take in introducing such a woman as my wife! Bosh! If you ever had such a idea in your head, abandon it at once. As for Lillian Fairchild, that is my business, and the half a million at stake only makes the game more interesting. So far as her consent, there's many a woman prefers marriage to something worse.

Kate. Is there nothing that will disuade you in your hellish determination?

Demp. Nothing! Rather than see Lillian Fairchild the wife of another, I would mingle our life-currents in a crimson stream and laugh defiance to God and man! Before she shall ever leave yonder dungeon other than my wife, her bones shall mingle with the dust of ruins, while the crimson tongue of the fiery demon shall feast upon all that is mortal of Lillian Fairchild.

Kate. Listen then. Lillian Fairchild shall never be your wife! Call it jealously, call it madness, call it what you will, but I warn you that within this hour I will turn you over to the authorities, the twice-ten-times criminal that you are! (*Dempsy advances, placing hand in vest.*) Strike, coward, if you dare! It will only add one more blood stain to your blackened soul, while it may spare me a few heartachs and a life of sorrow and degredation! (*Kate throus up her arm, baring her heart for his blow—Dempsy draws knife and is about to strike when Dude rushes in L 2, knocks the knife out of his hand with his umbrella, kicks it off stage R and belables Dempsy with umbrella driving him off R 2. During time, Kate Ex L 2. Dude becomes suddenly scart, faints and falls upon stage center.*)

Enters Mary Ann R 1.

M. A. (*Going to dude, sees that he has only fainted and brings him to consciousness.*) Sure Oi've found a dead mon—Naw, he's only losht his wind! No wather, no salts, no nothin' to bring him out. Wait a bit and Oi'll fich him out of it. (*Takes pin and sticks it into dude—jumping back.*)

Dude. (*Recovering rising and looking around as if in fear.*) Aw! Aw thot aw was hurt!

M. A. (*Going L—aside.*) Sure Oi thot twas a man all the while.

Dude. (*Seeing Mary Ann, begins desperate flirtation which pleases her.*) Aw! Ma dwear young ladaw!

Andy appears R 1.

(*Flirtation continued—Andy catches Dude by shoulders, shakes him thoroughly, hits him with knee, Dude dances and tries to get away— Andy runs him off L 3.*

Andy. Sure, Oi have a moind to shake the britches off of 'im! (*Sees Mary Ann L but goes R—pouting and looking over left shoulder.*)

M. A. (*Coming forward,*) Andy—Andy—Andy me bie! Did ye know that yer swate-heart was calling ye? (*Andy acts mad and won't look around—touches him on the arm.*) Andy, me darlint, was ye mad at yer own Mary Ann?

Andy. (*Jerking his shoulders.*) Go darlint the jude! Oi'm not yer darlint, Oi'm goin' to marry Biddy McFliggin, so Oi am!

M. A. Sure, Andy, me darlin, ye should not be angry wid yer own Mary. Ann gist becase she was havin' a bit o' fun wid a jude. Sure it was but a wee bit of a flirtation. (*Touching his ribs.*)

Andy. (*Jumping and laughing.*) O-ouch, Mary Ann, how can ye make me laugh whin me heart is breakin' for the loiks of ye!

M. A. Sure Oi knowd that ye'd not be angry all the whoile! Now hident ye bather ax me pardin' and make all up over again? (*Putting up cheek to be kissed.*)

Andy. (*Throwing arm around waist and drawing her to him.*) Sure, me darlint, makin' ope is for all the woruld loik sparkin' all over agin. (*Takes handkerchief, wipes a place on her cheek and kisses her.*) What say ye? Shall we have a bit of a song fer company loik?

M. A. Ald roit. me darlint, and Oi'll help ye out a bit.

(*Sings.*)

Andy.   If iver Oi marry, me darlint shall be
The swatest of women that iver ye sai,
Oi'll hug her and kiss her and love her so will
That she'll nivor repint it—Oi will, so Oi will.

Both dance   Tra tal de ral li da, tra tal de ral a
and sing.   Tra tal de ral li da, tra tal de ral e.
(*He*)   Oi'll hug her and kiss her and love her so will
That she niver'll repint it—Oi will, so Oi will.

M. A. If iver Oi marry, me darlint shall be ·
A true Irish bie from the isle o'er the sai;
And if he should squaze me, indade Oi'll not jump
Nor call for me mammy—Oi won't; no, Oi won't.

Both sing (Tra tol de ral li da, tra tal de ral a;
and dance. \ Tra tol de ral li da, tra tal de ral e,
(She) And if he should squaze me, indade Oi'll not jump
Nor call for me mammy—Oi won't; no, Oi won't.

Both. Thin whin we are married so happy we'll be
In our nate little cot—gist me darlint and me.

He. Oi'll save all me earnings to put in the till
And stay home ivery avening—Oi will, so Oi will.

She in (Oi niver will blame him—me darlint, me trump
concert.) Nor scold him for smokin'—Oi won't; no, Oi won't.

·) Tra tal de ral li da, tra tal de ral a;
Both.) Tra tal de ral li da, tra tal de ral e.

(*Both repeat their separate line s in concert.*)
*Fire-bell rings off R 3.

Andy. Sure, Mary Ann, there's goin' to be a fire, lets go to it!
(*Glow red light is seen off R 3.*) [*Both rush off R 2.*
Enters Dempsy R 3.

Demp. (*Looking back at fire.*) ˙ Ha, ha! Thwart my plans, will
they! Ere this, Lillian Fairchild is beyond the reach of human
assistance! [*Rushes off L 1.*
Enters Tom Weed L 2.

Tom. My God! The tenament is on fire! [*Rushes off R 3.*
Enters Kate Field L 3.

Kate. (*Sees fire, throws up hands—Fire grows brighter.*) Great
heavens! The dugeon is on fire! Lillian, Oh, Lillian! God deliver her from that wicked man! (*Starts off R 3, looks, throws up
hands.*) Thank God, she's saved!

Enters Tom Weed R 3, bearing Lillian unconscious in his arms.
Enters Jack Dempsy L 1, with drawn poniard.

Demp. (*Taking Weed by throat and swinging knife above his head.*)
Death to everyone that crosses my path! (*Weed tries to stay his
hand.*)
Enters Timothy Weed R. 2—rushing toward Dempsy and catches arm.
QUICK CURTAIN.

*SUGGESTION.—Ring fire-bell in covered box or barrel to give distance.

ACT IV.

SCENE 1. — *Tom Weed's new home. Mary Ann discovered with a duster in hand setting things to right — Singing.*

M. A. Sure Oi've dusted ivery room in the whole house, paled the preaties, set the bread to brewin' and got iverything ready for Miss Lillian and Mashter Wade's return from the schurch. Sure their's a foin pair as iver jumpped over the broom-stick and Oi hope that bloody Dempsy'll let them alone' so Oi do. He's a durthy blarguard as disarves hangin' an Oi hope the palace will git him yit, Oi shouldn't wander if hed be killin'some of us before they catch the loiks of him. Ah, here comes me darlint. (*Very busy with brush and does not look up.*)

Enters Andy R 1.

Andy. (*Throws kisses at Mary Ann, winks and tries to attract her attention. Finally jumps and catches her.*) Ouch, me darlint who's got ye now?

M. A. (*Screams.*) Och! for the loife of me, who is it that's skeerin' me out o' me wits! (*Leans heavily in his arms.*)

Andy. (*Straightening her up.*) Sure and the mashter said Oi should come ope and help yez about gitin' the dinner ready whoilst they wint for the parson.

M. A. Och, and is it dinner yer afther helpin' me wid! Sure the dinner is narely riddy aldready. (*Begins dusting again.*)

Andy. (*Sniffling.*) Sure Oi smil the chicken is burnin. (*Starts toward door rear.*)

M. A. (*Looking up.*) Oi say Andy!

Andy. What is it me darlint?

M. A. Was ye goin' out agin?

Andy. Gist to fix the faier, me swate-hart.

M. A. Thin when ye come back, gist scare me agin. (*Ex Andy rear.*) Sure that bie will tease the loife out of me.

Re-enters Andy rear, with chicken leg.

Andy. (*Eating.*) Oi say. Mary Ann; Yer chicken is a little too fresh.

M. A. (*Taking after him chasing him around stage with duster.*) Its no fresher than the loiks of ye, who'll be snoopin' in the pot for the bisht piece.

Andy. Sure, and Oi was only afther the wish-bone! The mashter would not care about th it, now. (*Looks off R. 2.*) Sure Mary Ann, the mashter is coming. (*Goes left and hides behind Mary Ann, picking bone rapidly.*)

Enters Tom, and Lillian in bridal robe, Mr. and Mrs. Weed, Kate and the dude. R. 1.

Tom. (*Taking her hands.*) Lillian, my wife, a thousand times welcome to our little home; none the less sacred for the terrible hours of torture—days that seemed an eternity of sorrow. It shall be a haven of rest and safety, where, surrounded by faithful and loving friends, my life shall be devoted to blotting out the memory of the terrible anguish my love has caused you.

Lil. Not your love, Tom; but the misfortune of being rich without knowing it. But I do not feel safe, even in this beautiful retreat as long as that wicked man is at liberty. Who knows but this very moment he might rush in upon us and carry out his awful threat.

Andy. (*Wiping his mouth on Mary Ann's apron, comes out of his hiding place and draws long knife from neck with difficulty and strikes defensive attitude.*) Let him come! Oi repate it sor, lit him come! (*Walks R. and L. across stage at "present arms."—Stops at Mary Ann's side L.*

Tom. There is no danger of that, Lillian, the officers are in hot persuit and he cannot long escape them. However I wish you were the poor girl I wooed and won, beyond the reach of evil this great wealth may throw around you.

Tim. I'll be tetotally consarned ef I dont think that boy's goin' crazy. (*Coming up and taking hold of Tom's arm.*) Don't be afferd of the money, Tom; it won't hurt ye a bit. Can find more'n forty men up in Vermont that'd take care of it fer ye, and not charge ye a cent. (*Aside.*) Don't know but I could help the boy out a little myself on a pinch.

Lil. (*Laughing.*) Oh, I don't doubt but we shall be able to find a way to take care of it, and make it a great blessing in caring for these friends who have befriended us in our hour of peril. (*Andy shakes money in pocket and looks wise.*)

Mrs. W. (*To Lillian.*) Yes, an' in buyin' dishes and things ter keep house with, an' close, an' so on—howsomever I've got a lot o' Tom's ol' close as aint entirely weard out yit, 'at 'ud do with a little darning now an' then.

Lil. Oh, thank you, mother, I am sure we shall do very nicely.

Tim. I say, Tom, ef yer goin' ter have dead loads o' money, yer mint all come up and spend a week at the Hollar. Yer ma an' me lows ter take this young gal out ter live with us in the Hollar, and the rest o' ye can gist as well go along.

Lil. Oh, no, no: father! I cannot consent to that just yet. Miss Field must remain with me until she overcomes this despondency and then we will talk about a trip to the country. Mary Ann must stay and help me about keeping the house, and I am sure we will get along very nicely.

Andy. And plase, mum, ye'll warnt ma to dhrive the chickens to wather?

Lil. Oh you will have to stay and watch Mary Ann.

Dude. (*Who has been standing near entrance R 1, biting end of umbrella.*) Aw do declawr! Quite left out Aw must sway.

Kate. Not entirely, Mr. Stibbins; you and I will go into the home missionary work, both having a most excellent subject; and perhaps through our own short-comings we may learn to be more charitable to others. (*Dude makes very low bow, takes her hand and touches it to his lips.*)

Tim. I'll be tetotally codsarned ef this aint gettin' jolly! Feel just as if I could dance a jig! Choose yer partners for the funny musk! (*Music starts up.*) All join hands and circle to the left!

Positions.

MRS. WEED, MR. WEED, LILLIAN, TOM,
R. KATE, DUDE,   MARY ANN, ANDY, L.

FIGURE: *Circle left—Chassez to sides—forward all—forward and pass through—Ladies change—half promenade—half right and left - chassez by couples—forward all—forward and pass through—*

ladies change - half promenade--half right and left—chassez by couple—forward all—forward again, form half circle and forward all --recede.

Gun is fired without—music ceases—Dempsy rushes in R 1. with drawn poniard, rushes to Lillian—Tom steps between, Mr. Weed fells Dempsy with left hand—Andy couches behind Mary Ann and begins to draw out long knife.

Tim. That's one I had LEFT.

Enters officers with revolvers in hand and captures Dempsy.

CURTAIN.

"Tangled Lives."

The dramatization of Barrett Sylvester's novel of same name by the author of "A SCRAP OF BROWN PAPER," is an Emotional Domestic Drama of great force. English costumes.